THE HAUNTED PLANET

by DJ Arneson and Tony Tallarico

Watermill Press

THE HAUNTED PLANET

Printed in the United States of America.

The Haunted Gull

The boy stood alone on the empty beach. Clutched tightly in his hand was a shiny new wooden bow. An arrow lay across the bow, notched and ready. Far down the beach, thirteen white and gray gulls glided over the waves as they broke with a hiss on the smooth wet sand. The boy watched the birds and waited. His fingers tightened on the bow.

The gulls soared closer. Their wings didn't move. They turned their heads from side to side as they skimmed the green edge of the endless ocean. The boy heard the gulls calling *kree, kree* over the rumbling thunder of the tumbling waves. He dropped to his belly on the hot sand and waited for them.

The first of the scavenging birds swooped over the boy's head. Another followed, and then another. The boy rolled onto his side. He clenched the bow in one hand. He pulled the string back as far as it would go with the other.

The birds soared on. By ones and twos they skimmed the water. Tiny fish leaped in frenzy ahead of the birds' sharp beaks. Most survived. Those which didn't were carried aloft and eaten on the wing.

The boy got up on one knee. He pointed the brass tip of his arrow at the scattered flight and let go of the string.

The arrow whistled. The bowstring hummed. The last gull turned its head toward the sound. Its wings flashed. They rose and fell with powerful strokes on the wind. But the arrow was faster. It struck the bird.

A crimson stain spread over the bird's snow-white breast. Its wings fluttered weakly. The bird fell to earth behind a low dune.

The boy stood. He was alone on the empty beach. He stared in disbelief at what he had done.

"I didn't mean to," he said.

He let the bow drop. He walked slowly to the dune where the bird fell. He paused at the top. He was afraid to take the last step. He was afraid to see what he had done.

The bird wasn't there. The boy stumbled down the side of the dune through ankle-deep sand. Tiny windswept ripples lay in an unbroken pattern around the base of the dune.

The arrow lay on the sand like a stick floating on the ocean. Its tip was bright red.

Kree. Kree.

The boy looked up. The sun was ablaze in the sky.

A dark shadow crossed swiftly in front of the fiery disc. The boy covered his eyes. When he looked again, the sky was empty.

"I didn't mean to," he said.

That night the boy lay alone in his bed. The room was as dark as the midnight sky. The sough of the ocean was far, far off. It sounded like a distant moan. The boy's eyes were open wide. They rolled from side to side from one deep shadow on the wall to another. The boy watched the shadows and didn't move.

Something bumped on top of the roof. The boy stared at the dark ceiling. The room was still.

A faint, tap, tapping moved from one side of the roof to the other. It stopped. It returned to where it started. The tapping passed back and forth, back and forth over the boy's head.

The boy clutched his covers. He pulled them to his neck. He didn't move his head. He didn't close his eyes. He watched the shadowy ceiling as the tapping noise walked along the roof.

"I didn't mean to," he whispered.

The tapping stopped.

The boy held his breath.

"I really didn't mean to," the boy gasped.

The roof was silent.

"What are you going to do to me?" the boy said.

Something fluttered over the roof.

The boy turned his head toward the dark window in the deepest shadow of the room. He moved so slowly the covers didn't rustle.

A sharp rap sounded against the glass. It was as crisp as a pebble striking the windowpane. The glass clattered again and again. The harsh sound of pecking filled the room.

The boy jammed his pillow around his ears.

The sound grew louder.

The window cracked. Glass exploded into the room in a shower of brilliant diamonds of starlight. They sprinkled to the floor and then went out.

The boy sat up straight. His wide eyes blinked rapidly. He stuck his head deep into the darkness to see.

Stars twinkled in the moonless sky through the shattered window. They vanished one by one as a shadow moved in front of them.

The boy's chest heaved up and down. He sobbed.

The shadow in the window moved. It whistled on the wind. It was in the room.

The boy shook.

Sharp claws scratched against the wooden rail at the foot of the boy's bed. The scratching moved back and forth. The boy followed the sound with his eyes.

The thing fluttered. The air whistled. The stars in the sky blinked as the shadow swooped out of the window and was gone.

The boy leaped out of bed. He raced across the pitch black floor to a crack of light coming from beneath the bedroom door.

The boy threw open the door.

"Mommy! Daddy!" he screamed.

The small seaside cabin was a shambles. Broken furniture lay in smashed heaps on the floor. Ripped drapes hung in long ragged shreds from smashed windows. Sharp crystals of broken glass lay everywhere.

The screen door hung awkwardly from a broken hinge. The screen was torn wide open as if something had burst into the room from outside. Bits of downy white feathers clung to the ragged wire screen like unmelted flakes of snow.

The boy froze. He stared into the unblinking beady black eyes of twelve white and gray gulls perched atop the destruction around him like a circle of hungry vultures. Their beaks were stained crimson.

"Mommy? Daddy?"

Something fluttered outside in the darkness over the cabin. It landed on the roof with a bump.

Kree. Kree, it called.

The gulls closed their circle around the terrified boy.

In the morning the cabin was boarded up. The "For Rent" sign over the door was taken down. A deputy sheriff drove the dusty station wagon with out-of-state license plates down the sandy driveway behind two long, somber black cars.

A cool, damp wind blew in from the sea. It riffled the dry marsh grass clinging to the low dunes in front of the abandoned cabin.

Thirteen white and gray gulls lined the peak of the house with wings open wide to the wind.

One by one the gulls hopped into the breeze. They tucked their feet under their streamlined bodies and glided toward the shore.

The last bird circled the house on silent wings. It cocked its head at the caravan of grim vehicles moving far down the lonely beach road.

The bird soared high into the sky. It rose in a sweeping arc, higher and higher until the crimson stain on its snow white breast blended with the fiery red disc of the blazing morning sun.

Kree. Kree, it called.

And then it was gone.

The Empty Motel

The question was, why was the motel empty?

Bob Potter set the parking brake of his family station wagon, but left the engine running. The windshield wipers flopped back and forth across the rain-streaked windshield. Brilliant strokes of hot lightning scorched across the sky, leaping from black cloud to black cloud and sizzling to the windswept ground. Potter wiped his hand across the glass to see through the storm.

On the hillside above the parking lot stood the motel. It was a very large building to be so far in the country. Three stories tall, it looked as if it were meant to sit on the downtown street of a small city.

The building was constructed of brick and stone and looked very much like an English castle. Large stained-glass windows stared down at the rain-soaked parking lot like giant eyes. Tall towers rose from each corner of the block-long motel.

"There must be three hundred rooms in that monster," Bob Potter said to his wife on the seat next to him.

Laurie Potter put her finger to her lips. "Shh. The girls are still sleeping."

In the back seat of the car lay Susan and Debbie Potter in twisted heaps amid the mess and clutter of a long car trip. Hamburger wrappers, empty milkshake cups, and an assortment of flopped open comic books littered the seat.

Behind the girls in the suitcase-stuffed rear of the car, Muffin, Susan's tiny white poodle, blinked her pink, watery eyes.

"I'll bet there are more than three hundred rooms in that thing," Bob Potter whispered. He wiped the fog from the windshield again for a fresh look at the ominous building on the hill.

"All we need is one," Laurie said.

"Wait in the car. I'll run up there, get us registered and come back for you. No sense in all of us getting wet if we don't have to."

Potter slipped out the door. He cast a curious look at his wife just before closing it. "What I can't figure out is why we're the only car here."

Laurie smiled. "Hurry up," she said. "You'll catch your death in that cold rain."

Potter loped across the broad parking lot to the front entrance of the unusual building. Laurie watched him from the dry comfort of the car. She turned on the car heater. Even though it was summer and they were on vacation, the sudden thunderstorm had chilled the air. The heater felt good to the young mother, who was dressed only in shorts and a simple shirtwaist.

Rain drummed on the car roof. Laurie looked at her watch and shook her head. She wiped a clear circle on the steamy windshield and squinted through the growing darkness at the motel. "What could be taking him so long?" she wondered.

Five more minutes passed. Laurie Potter grew increasingly nervous. She fidgeted in the seat. The air in the car was stuffy. A thin strand of tiny beads of sweat formed on her brow. She creased her forehead to squint through the gloom of night that was fast descending on the forsaken motel and its huge, empty lot. The sweat trickled down her face. The back of her shirt stuck damply to the seat. Her hands trembled.

The sky was solid black. Thunderclouds joined together overhead to close off the sky completely.

Rain pelted the solitary car sitting between two white stripes painted on the vast, black parking lot.

Laurie turned off the engine. The wipers stopped their monotonous swishing and flopping. While thunder bellowed like angry bulls around her, the inside of the car was as silent as a tomb.

"For goodness sake, Bob. Hurry back. *Please.*"

"Mommy?"

Laurie swallowed hard. Her attention was riveted on the grim motel. Susan's sudden cry made her jump.

"I'm here, darling."

"Where's daddy?"

Laurie looked back at the silent motel. There were no lights in any of the hundreds of windows. No sign flickered above the door bidding welcome to weary travelers as other motels on their route had. Only when the white flash of a lightning bolt split the sky was it possible to see the place clearly.

"He--uh--he's getting us a room, sweetheart."

Debbie sat up next to her older sister and rubbed her eyes.

Susan wiped a tiny hole in the steam-covered window and put her eye to it as if she were looking for a mouse that lived inside. "In there?" she asked.

Mrs. Potter tried to smile but she couldn't. "Mmmm hmmm."

"I don't like that place," Susan said. "It's just like my dream."

Laurie shuddered. "He'll be right back, girls," she said.

"I have to go to the bathroom."

"Me, too."

Mrs. Potter wiggled around to face the girls.

"Can it wait until Dad comes back?" she said.

"What about Muffin?"

"What about her?"

"She's nervous."

Mrs. Potter wiped the sweat from her brow. Her hand felt clammy. Her heart beat unevenly. "Please girls. All of you. Everything will just have to wait until. . .until Dad gets back."

"It's stuffy in here."

"Open a window."

Laurie jumped. "No. Girls. Don't. It's pouring out and---"

Debbie, nearest the window facing the motel, had already rolled a window halfway down. Before she could crank it up, Muffin leaped over the back of the seat, bounced out of Susan's lap and popped out the window.

"Muffin!"

The tiny dog scampered across the lot straight for the motel. It stopped at the front door and began to yip loudly, though the sound could not carry through the downpour and thunder.

The door opened from inside. The dog disappeared.

17

"This is ridiculous, girls. We've waited out here long enough. Come on. We're going in."

Laurie Potter held an open road map over her head. She waited until Susan and Debbie were ready. Then both car doors flew open and the three leaped out.

"Run," Mrs. Potter shouted.

The girls scooted across the lot. They splashed through puddles on the way, laughing and screaming like puppies put out to play. The mother followed them, stepping briskly around the puddles, but never taking her eyes off the darkened motel front door.

Laurie pulled open the door. Debbie and Susan scurried in behind her. They stomped up and down to shake the water from their sneakers.

"It's empty," Laurie Potter said. Her voice sounded hollow.

"Where's daddy?"

Susan and Debbie clung to their mother's wet legs. The three stood in a puddle of water which had dripped from them onto the floor. The floor was rough, unfinished cement. The walls of the inside of the building were the same.

The Potter women stood in the dark entry of a cavernous, uncompleted, very empty, three-story tall motel lobby. Twisted copper electrical wires stuck out of the walls like angry metal snakes. Boards and bricks lay everywhere. The smell of damp cement and musty earth filled the place.

Laurie Potter couldn't move. Her body

trembled and shook. Her teeth chattered from cold and fear.

There was no trace of Bob Potter. There was no trace of anyone at all in the ugly, awful, dead shell of a building.

"Bob!"

"Bob. . .Bob. . .Bob. ."

The echo of Laurie's worried shout dimmed to a hush.

"I. .it's empty. There's nobody here," Mrs. Potter said.

"No it's not, mommy."

Susan tugged her mother's arm. "There's a man back there," she said.

"What are you talking about?"

"It's just like my dream, mommy, just like I told you."

Susan started across the floor toward the shadowy rear of the hollow, unfinished lobby.

"Susan."

"It's o.k., mommy. He doesn't want *me*."

Laurie Potter leaped two steps over the rough cement and grabbed Susan by the arm. Debbie was clamped tightly in her other hand.

"Ouch. You're hurting me."

"Me, too."

Mrs. Potter kneeled beside her daughters and held them close. "I don't know what dream you're talking about, but I want you to stop this instant. Do you hear me?"

Susan began to frown. Then her face lighted up. She pointed to the shadows. "There he is," she said.

"Is it da. . .?"

Mrs. Potter rose slowly to her feet. Her eyes were big and wide. They didn't blink. They were fixed on a murky figure that emerged from the shadows of the cave-like room.

It wasn't Bob Potter.

Susan pulled herself free from her mother's grip. "It's o.k.," she said. "He doesn't want me. He already told me so in my dream."

Susan walked unafraid toward the figure in the shadows. "Can I have Muffin back now? You promised."

A low moan came from the figure.

"Well, where is she then?"

The figure moaned again.

"What about my daddy? Is he sleeping too?"

Laurie shuddered. Icy prickles skittered up and

down her bare legs and arms.

Susan walked slowly back to her mother and sister. Her lips were tightly pursed in a pout. "He's not like the one in my dream," she said. "The one in my dream said I could have Muffin back." She turned to the figure. "You're *mean.*"

Two ruby red lights blinked from the top of the figure in the darkness. Eyes.

"What are you? What have you done with my husband?"

Laurie let go of Debbie and ran toward the shadow. She plunged in the darkness deep inside the hollow lobby shell.

"Mommy!"

Laurie Potter was gone.

"I want to go home."

Debbie put her thumb into her mouth and lowered her head so she couldn't see the shadow.

Susan stood alongside her. She set her feet firmly on the rough floor. "What did you do with my mommy and daddy and my little sister's dog Muffin?" she said. "I'm not going until you tell me. You lied. In my dream you said we could all go home. You're a *liar,* that's what you are."

The eyes in the shadow blinked again and then they were gone. The shadow melted into the surrounding darkness.

The girls were alone.

"Where's daddy?"

"He's in a room."

"How do you know?"

"'Cause it was in my dream."

"Which room?"

"I don't know. There are lots."

"Are we gonna look?"

Susan arched her head back so she could look straight up at the ceiling above her. "I guess so," she said.

The two little girls wandered hand in hand down a long, empty black corridor on the top floor of the strange motel. They paused at each door which lined the sides of the tunnel-like hallway and knocked.

"Mommy? Daddy?"

Low moans from inside the rooms replied.

The girls moved on to the next room.

"Does he want me, too?" Debbie asked.

Susan tightened her grip on her sister's tiny hand. "No," she said. "He doesn't want me and he doesn't want you. He said so in my dream."

"But you said he lied already."

"I know."

"Who does he want then?"

"I don't know."

"Does he want mommy and daddy?"

"I guess so."

"Is he gonna keep them?"

"I don't know."

"Who is he?"

"I don't know."

"Is he keeping everybody in these rooms?"

"I don't know."

Susan stopped in front of the next door. She knocked sharply. "Daddy? Mommy?"

There was no reply.

"Is he a ghost?"

"Don't be silly. There's no such thing as ghosts."

"How do you know?"

"I just know."

"Then what is he?"

"I told you I don't know."

Debbie pulled her hand free. They had reached the last door. The little girl pounded her small clenched fists against it with all her might.

Yip. Yip. Yip.

"It's Muffin," Debbie shouted. "He's in there."

The door creaked open. A dull red light glowed from inside. The two girls stepped into the room. A gust of icy wind blew the door closed behind them with a roar that shook the building. The light in the room went out and the motel was as silent as the grave.

The answer was, the motel wasn't *empty.*

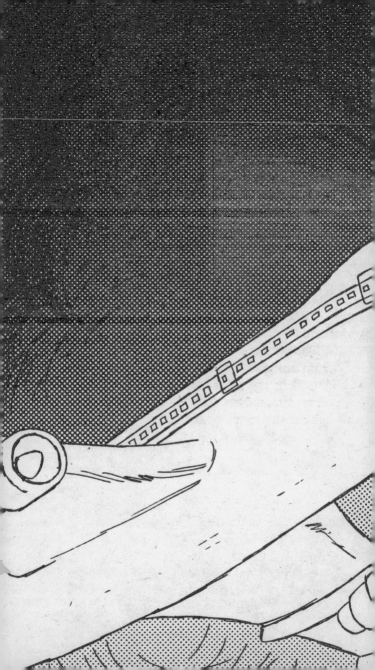

Ghost Flight

"Your flight path will take you directly through the Bermuda Triangle."

Airline Captain Buzz Arnold shrugged his shoulders.

"So?"

Penny Alvarez, in charge of Sea Central Airline's Flight Operations Desk leaned over the counter separating her from the pilots and flight crews milling about on the other side. She smiled coyly at Buzz Arnold. "So I just thought you ought to know, that's all."

She handed him a sheaf of papers neatly clipped to a metal board. "It's my job to provide you with flight planning. If there's anything unusual I think you should know about, I tell you." She waved a hand toward the other pilots and crew. "All of you, Captain. So don't think there's anything special about the fact that I told you."

Arnold riffled through the papers and handed the board back to Penny Alvarez.

"As far as I'm concerned, today's flight is just like any other and our route is just like any other, too. I don't care if I'm supposed to fly through The Bermuda Triangle, the Devil's Kitchen or the Big Bad Wolf's Woods. I fly where the company tells me to fly."

Arnold, a ruggedly handsome man with square shoulders, steel blue eyes and silver gray streaks in the jet black hair that showed beneath the uniform cap sitting jauntily atop his head, stepped away from the counter. His copilot, First Officer Lem Calhoun, and their Flight Engineer, Biff Bolt, joined him at the door.

The three paused as Arnold called back to Penny Alvarez over the din of the busy office.

"And I know all about the so-called Bermuda Triangle, Miss Alvarez. I've got two teen-agers and one sixth grader who have just about bored my ears off with stories about its *mysteries*."

The captain forced a very serious-looking frown, but the twinkle in his eye could not be hidden.

"However, if I run into anything unusual, you'll be the first to know. I'll call you right away on the company radio."

"It's *Ms* Alvarez, Captain. And if you'd been listening to your kids, you'd know that if you run into anything unusual in the Bermuda Triangle, it's already too late."

"What was that all about?"

Biff Bolt, the youngest of the flight crew, hurried to keep pace with the two pilots as the three walked swiftly toward their departure gate and the huge, silver-sided, wide body jet waiting for them there.

"Stuff and nonsense," Arnold said. "We've been diverted from our regular flight path because of Hurricane Bruce. The new course puts us right across comic book country."

Bolt shoved his cap back and scratched his head. "Comic book country?"

"The Bermuda Triangle," Arnold said. "Where all the stories in my kids' comics seem to come from."

Lem Calhoun grinned.

Biff Bolt didn't.

Sea Central Flight 222 broke through the overcast into a brilliant, sunlit sky. Towering pillars of gray-black clouds a hundred miles away on the horizon were the nearest signs of the killer hurricane sweeping up the coast.

"Sea Central two-two-two requests permission to climb to three fiver."

The radio speaker on the flight deck of the streaking jetliner crackled.

"Sea Central two-two-two cleared for flight level three fiver. Over."

Captain Arnold scanned the horizon as the plane leveled off at thirty-five thousand feet.

"It'll be good to get some of that Caribbean sunshine after the rain we've been having."

Lem Calhoun nodded.

"That hurricane is messing up my kids' vacations. I wish it would blow through and get it over with."

The men in the cockpit chatted as the giant airliner streaked through the sky. The ocean beneath them was obscured by the thick layer of clouds churned up by Hurricane Bruce. In the passenger section, two-hundred and eighty-seven people read, snacked and slept as the minutes became an hour and an hour became two.

The airplane flew in the shadow of giant thunderheads which rose so high above it that their tops were lost from view.

Lem Calhoun craned his neck to the window and looked up.

"Out of sight. Absolutely out of sight."

Biff Bolt's sharp eyes scanned the dozens of

dials and gauges which surrounded his desk behind the two flight officers. A flicker of a meter needle caught his attention. It held steady. Then it flickered again. Bolt tapped the meter with a fingertip. The needle didn't move.

"I think we'll give those clouds a little more distance," Captain Arnold said.

Arnold and Calhoun fixed their eyes on the boiling black clouds off their right wingtip. The plane curved away from the giants, but the powerful forces of nature inside the cauldrons kept pace with the plane.

"They seem to be following us, Captain."

Arnold studied the peculiar clouds. "There's no way a storm can travel five-hundred-and-twenty-seven knots," he said. "We'll outrun 'em. Don't worry."

Another needle on Biff Bolt's control panel jiggled. Then another.

"Cap'n, I've got some kind of power aberration back here."

In the passenger cabin a bored young boy fidgeted with his earphones as he gazed blankly out the window at the churning clouds. He twisted the channel selector dial on his armrest. His eyes lighted up.

"Hey, Dad. Listen to this."

"Later, Son. I've got work to do."

The boy put the earphones back on.

"Fighter pilots. Wow."

All of the needles on Biff Bolt's panels

shivered. They flopped back and forth across their lighted dial faces like tiny windshield wipers. Then the lights began to flicker.

"Can you trace the problem?"

Biff Bolt expertly turned knobs and set switches.

"Negative, Cap'n. All the internal systems are clean. It seems to be coming from outside the aircraft."

The boy in the passenger cabin pressed his nose to the window.

"Wow. Dad. Look. There they are. Five of them. Fighters."

"I'm busy, Son."

Lem Calhoun stared in disbelief out his window.

"Captain?"

Arnold saw them too. He hit the microphone switch on his control yoke with his thumb.

"Radar control. Sea Central two-two-two. Are you controlling a five-plane formation off our starboard wing?"

The radio speaker crackled sharply.

"Negative, Sea Central two-two-two. We've got you on our scope at three fiver. You're alone."

First Officer Lem Calhoun's eyes widened. "The Devil we are," he gasped.

The radio speaker crackled again. Then it went dead.

"Radio power is out, sir."

Arnold turned quickly to Bolt.

"Switch over to emergency power."

"I did, Cap'n. That's gone too."

The three men in the cockpit faced the right hand windows. Outside, silhouetted against the lightning flashes in the billowing hurricane clouds were the sharp, distinct images of five airplanes. The silhouettes grew larger and larger as the planes turned in a graceful arc toward the giant airliner.

"Captain. For the love of Pete. *Do you see what they are?*"

The planes swooped like streaking bullets across the nose of the jet. Arnold yanked back on the yoke to avoid a collision.

"Avengers, Captain. Those airplanes are World War Two Avengers. Torpedo planes. . . over thirty-five years old."

The strange, midnight blue planes were gone.

"They're coming back, Dad. I can hear them talking. Did you see them? They went right in front of us."

"I'm trying to write this report. . ."

"But, Dad. Those old-fashioned planes. . ."

"Calvin."

"Oh, o.k."

The boy held the channel selector switch halfway between two numbers. He scanned the dark sky outside the window as he listened.

"Avenger flight leader to captain of commercial airliner. Avenger flight leader to captain of commercial airliner. Do you read me?"

"I wonder why our pilot doesn't answer?" the boy said. He continued to watch the sky for the reappearance of the unusual airplanes.

"Commercial airliner. Commercial airliner. You are approaching an area of extreme danger. Turn back. Turn back. Commercial airliner. Do you read me?"

Captain Arnold held the control yoke tightly in his hands. He twisted his head from side to side, looking from one window to the other. "Do you see them?"

Calhoun shook his head.

"Anything new with the radios?"

Biff Bolt didn't look up from his panel. His fingers flew from switch to button to dial.

"Negative."

Suddenly the alien planes were alongside. A blue aura of electricity shimmered over the dark painted surfaces. Their greenhouse-like canopies were frosted over, but inside each plane was the unmistakable shadow of a pilot at the controls.

"Commercial airliner. Turn back. Turn back. You are less than five miles from the edge. Turn back."

The boy at the window sat on his knees for a better look at the black flight gliding swiftly and soundlessly alongside the jam-packed jet.

"Nobody's answering them, Dad. They're trying to talk to us but nobody's talking back. Should I go up in the front and tell the pilot or something?"

The boy's father's nose was buried in paperwork. "Later, Calvin. I'm busy."

The lead plane suddenly peeled away from the flight. One by one the following planes flashed their sleek undersides at the jet and flopped over onto their backs in a sweeping, follow-the-leader turn.

"How are those things keeping up with us?" Arnold said. "Their top speed is under two-fifty knots."

"Where did they come from?"

"The question is, what kind of idiots are they to endanger a plane load of passengers?"

Arnold was irate. His thumb flicked the microphone switch off and on, but the radios remained dead.

"They're attacking."

The flight of ancient warplanes roared in from out of the glow of the storm which was directly ahead of the jet. Flickers of orange fire blazed from their wings and spurts of blue smoke trailed behind.

"They're *strafing* us."

Arnold twisted the yoke. The huge plane sliced sharply to the left. The attacking planes turned to meet it. The jet turned farther away.

"You are two miles from the zone. Turn back. Turn back."

"What on earth is our pilot doing?"

"He's trying to get away from those planes, Dad. They're shooting at us so we'll turn back. We're heading straight into the zone. They even said so."

The boy's father looked up from his papers. He adjusted his moon-shaped reading glasses on his nose. He glanced at the movie screen at the front of the cabin. It was blank.

"Are you watching a movie or listening to a television show or what?"

"It's the old airplanes. They're attacking us so we won't fly into the zone."

"Honestly, Calvin. What am I going to do with you?"

The Avengers streaked by the jet. The giant jet was unaffected by their turbulence. It flew rock-steady under Captain Arnold's experienced hands as if there had been no airplanes there.

"Try the company radio frequency, Bolt."

Flight Engineer Bolt's hands flew over the console.

"I have the frequency, sir. But it's dead. Like all the others."

The Avengers swooped so close to the nose of the jet that Calhoun threw his arms in front of his face as if they would collide. But the strange planes hung off his wingtip, keeping steady pace with the jet as it streaked closer and closer to the lightning-filled cloud directly in its path.

"You've got less than a mile to turn. Turn back. Turn back."

The boy pressed the side of his head to his window so he could see ahead of the plane. The Avengers clung like pilot fish to the jet's steady course toward the glowing clouds.

"I think we're going into the Bermuda Triangle, Dad. I think that's what the zone is."

The boy uncurled his legs from under him and sat down on the seat. His head dropped to his chest.

"I'm afraid."

The Avengers arced over the top of the jet as it pierced the electric aura surrounding the darkest of the clouds. They soared over the top of the cloud as the airliner disappeared inside.

"They're gone, Captain."

Arnold stared in frozen silence through the windshield of his jet. His hands clenched the control yoke. His thumb was jammed down on the microphone button.

"We're caught in it. The controls are jammed. I can't turn the plane. We're trapped in the. . ."

Penny Alvarez stared at the silent radio speaker in the Flight Operations Office. Gathered around her were a dozen stunned co-workers.

"They crashed in the hurricane," a flight planner said in the hushed silence.

Penny Alvarez turned away from the fear-frozen group. She shook her head sadly.

"No. They didn't crash," she said. "It's not the hurricane."

Twelve heads turned slowly toward their young, stark-eyed boss.

"What is it then?"

Penny Alvarez shook her head from side to side.

"It. . .it's a place Captain Arnold calls. . . comic book country."

"How long are we going to be here, Dad?"

Calvin's earphones were silent. The giant jet's engines were silent. There was no sound anywhere.

The father sat upright in his seat staring blankly ahead.

The boy clambered out of his seat and stepped into the aisle. He walked slowly to the back of the plane. On either side sat stiff-backed men and women and children. Two-hundred and eighty-six of them. Their eyes were blank and lifeless, staring blindly ahead at nothing.

"I'm the only one that knows. I'm the only one."

Calvin returned to his seat and sat down. He put the earphones back on.

"Why don't they ever listen to us, Avenger flight leader?" the earphones crackled. "Why don't they ever listen?"

Calvin sniffed loudly. He wiped his eyes. He placed the earphones on his lap and turned to the window.

The Avengers were there. They would always be there.

Forever.

The Bridge

DO NOT CROSS BRIDGE AFTER DARK

The sign was so old the letters were hard to read. To a newcomer in town the weathered piece of wood nailed at a crazy angle didn't look like a sign at all. It hung on a rusty spike pinned to a wooden girder on the town side of the bridge. Across the narrow river was the park.

"Why aren't you supposed to cross at night?"

"Because the sign says so."

"That's no reason."

"Then I don't know."

"Can you cross in the daytime?"

"How else are you supposed to get to the park?"

"I don't know. You're the one that lives here. Not me."

"You live here."

"Yeah. For two weeks. But you've been here all your life."

"So?"

"So you should know something about something."

"I do. Plenty."

"Then why aren't you supposed to cross the bridge after dark?"

Jeff Tyler bit his lip. He squeezed the red plastic grips on his bike handlebars so hard that the knuckles on his hands turned white. He jerked the bike away from the bridge.

"Let's get out of here."

"I thought you were going to show me the park."

"I changed my mind. I'm going home."

Jeff kicked his leg over the seat and came down pedalling.

"Hey. Wait for me."

Joey Newcomb ran alongside his own bike to get up speed. He hopped from the ground to the seat like a cowboy mounting a runaway horse.

"Jeff. Wait up."

Jeff let his bike coast.

"What happened? I thought we were going to the park."

"I told you I changed my mind."

"Is it because of the bridge? Because I asked about the sign, I mean?"

Jeff stared straight ahead. His hair whipped away from his forehead and fluttered over his shoulders like streaks of flame. He started pumping hard again. He pulled away from Joey easily.

Joey's legs whirled like the blades of an electric fan. Sweat streamed down his face. He caught up to Jeff but he didn't have the energy to stay there. He let himself coast.

"Go on home, then. See if I care."

Joey turned back toward the bridge. He looked over his shoulder as Jeff vanished around a corner, still pedalling at top speed.

"I'll go to the park by myself. If it's dark or not."

He checked the sky. The sun was still very high. He breathed a sigh of relief as he caught his breath from the workout on the bike. He had no intention of going anywhere after dark in a town he barely knew.

Joey laid his bike in the grass near the end of the bridge. Voices from excited players in a baseball game in the park drifted across the river. The bridge was empty, but the park wasn't.

The bridge was an old-fashioned structure. A footbridge, it was just wide enough for three people to cross side by side. It was suspended over the river by two thick, rusty cables hanging from stone towers at each end. The towers rested on fat concrete bases which were buried in the river bed. Water swirled around the bases to make a gurgling noise which rose and fell in a steady rhythm.

"Maybe you aren't supposed to cross at night because it's so rickety."

Joey studied the bridge. The cables supporting the bridge were rusty. The wooden beams were scaly with ragged bits of old paint as rough as the bark of a tree. And the cement bases holding the whole thing up were definitely worn where the water rushed around them.

"That's got to be it. It's dangerous to walk on that thing at night."

Joey crossed the bridge. He stopped exactly halfway and hung over the rail to stare down at the foamy water. A board with a shiny black turtle on it drifted by, turning slowly in the current.

"I wonder if turtles get dizzy?"

Joey stopped in the park to watch the ballgame. He didn't know anybody on either team. He was too new in town. He bought a bag of peanuts at a homemade refreshment stand near the ball field and wandered deeper into the park.

"It's an island. I didn't know that."

Joey ate the last of his peanuts standing on the bank of another narrow, but quickly moving river. It was identical to the river on the opposite side of the park, except there was no bridge. He clambered down the rocky bank to the water's edge. The water was muddy, but its surface reflected his face. He dropped a pebble into the middle of his reflection. It shattered like liquid glass. The current smoothed it over. When the ripples were gone, Joey was staring into another face, a face with hollow eyes.

It wasn't his face.

A cold wind hit Joey across the back. His damp t-shirt clung like a layer of clammy ice to his shoulders. He leaped back from the reflection.

The reflection didn't move. It stayed on the surface of the running water, staring up at Joey through hollow, unblinking eyes. The mouth moved open and closed like a huge fish gasping for breath.

Joey whirled around. He scampered for footing on the greasy slope.

"Help! Help!"

His sneaker slipped off a muddy rock. His head snapped back. He shot his arms skyward and grasped the empty air with clawing fingers as he reeled backwards. He landed with a dull thud on the slippery bank. His head bounced off a half buried rock.

Joey Newcomb lay unconscious in the mud. His head was less than a foot away from the hollow-eyed face in the water. The mouth on the face moved.

Eeeeyyaaaahhhhhhhh.

Hours later a thin crescent moon trickled a meager ray of cold yellow light through the trees lining the river bank.

"Ohhhhhh."

Joey moved. His eyes opened. The sky above his head was as black as the river that bubbled in the darkness behind him. The park was as still as death.

"Help me."

Joey struggled to his feet. His knees were weak. His feet slipped on the slimy soil. He dropped to his hands and knees and scurried up the bank like a muskrat bound for home.

The park was empty. Beyond the other side, through the trees and across the opposite river, sparkled the lights of town.

Joey began to run. He raced through the darkness guided by the twinkling lights. Low branches slashed at him from out of the night as if he were surrounded by an army of invisible demons armed with slicing swords and stinging whips.

"Help! Please, somebody! Help me!"

The boy plunged through the velvet black shadows, on and on, stumbling but daring not to fall.

He burst into the broad clearing in the center

of the park where the ball diamond lay. The open space was a lake of night surrounded by black, scraggly tree shadows. Overhead, in a sky as dark as the earth beneath his feet, was the thin moon, surrounded by an icy burst of sparkling stars like brilliant flakes of distant snow.

Joey didn't slow down. He ran past the refreshment shack without a sideways glance. It was boarded shut and dark. A pungent whiff of bright yellow mustard from inside carried on a cushion of midnight wind was the only reminder that anyone else had ever been on the forsaken island.

Joey found the path, a ribbon of ink which twisted like a shadowy serpent through the trees. The lights on the other side of the river grew brighter. There were more of them. A church bell and a car horn sounded over the gurgling bubble of the rushing river and then were swallowed again.

A towering shadow loomed high into the sky blocking the stars and moon.

The bridge.

Joey threw his arms in front of him as if he were going to be hit. He braced his feet. His sneakers skidded across the pebbled path. He tripped and fell. He landed an arm's length away from the bridge.

Joey raised his face from the dust. The sour taste of blood filled his mouth. He swallowed rather than spit and make noise. His tongue gingerly touched the bleeding gash in his lip cut by his teeth.

The bridge was silhouetted against the flickering lights of town and the miniature dots of starlight in the sky. The tall pillars holding the cables stood like silent sentries on each side of the empty bridge.

Joey got to his knees. His heart pounded beneath his dirty, sweat-soaked shirt. The noise thundered in his ears. It grew louder as he staggered to his feet, like the sound of jungle drums spreading an urgent message across a forbidden place.

Joey placed a quivering foot on the bridge. Then another. He stood on the wood platform.

A wind roared across the bridge. Bitter cold and blowing hard, it whipped through the metal rails to make them howl and scream. The bridge quaked. It swayed from side to side as if pushed by a giant, unseen hand. Yet the leaves in the trees over Joey's head were still as a painting and no dust lifted from the quiet path behind him.

"Help me."

His tiny cry was much too weak to be heard over the roaring wind.

"Help me. Please. Somebody."

Joey's foot moved. Slowly, carefully, it glided forward and stopped. Then the other followed. Walking stiff and upright as if his joints were mired in solid grease, he stumbled forward, step by step. Though the raging wind continued to roar around him filling the air with a whistling shriek, it didn't touch him nor could he feel it.

The man with the hollow eyes was there. He stood flat-footed in the center of the bridge. He cast no shadow. The dim lights of town glowed behind him, straight through his body.

The man's arm rose shoulder high as if lifted by a helium balloon. The wrinkled, horribly twisted hand uncurled. A sharp finger without flesh beckoned to Joey.

Joey stumbled forward. His mouth hung open. His eyes were glazed. His long, jet black hair stood straight up. It turned completely white, surrounding his head like the gray cloud of a colossal ripe dandelion.

Step by step Joey drew closer and closer to the wildly grinning specter in the center of the bridge.

Eeeeyaaaaahhhhh.

The wind howled, but even its shrill scream wasn't loud enough to bury the wraith's cry.

The creature leaped. He threw his bony arms around Joey. The ragged ends of his shirt wrapped and tangled themselves around Joey's arms.

Joey struggled. He kicked and screamed. He beat his fists against the man's sunken chest. The dull, hollow thud of the grave echoed over the stinging shriek of the wind.

"Help! Help! Somebody help me! Dad! Daddy! Mommy! *Maaaaaaaaa. . ."*

The figure threw himself to the floor of the

bridge and rolled round and round with the kicking, struggling, screaming boy coiled tightly in his bony arms.

The wind stopped howling. The bridge stopped quaking. The man was gone.

And so was Joey.

"Here's his bike, you guys. Over here."

Jeff picked Joey's bike from the grass. He held it by the handlebars as two other boys joined him.

They stood in a tight circle around the bike. The sun was high in the sky. Shouts and screams from a ball game in the park drifted through the trees on a pleasant wind that smelled of mustard.

Jeff looked at the bridge. The sign hung awkwardly from its rusty spike, its letters no more legible than they were the day before. The rusty cables still needed paint and below, at the surface of the rushing water, the cement showed signs of wear.

And inside the thick base of the bridge, frozen in agony since the day the cement was poured, was the mummified body of a man who had fallen into the wet grip of tons of quickly hardening concrete, never to appear again—alive.

"Maybe I should have told him."

Jeff leaned over the rail as the muddy water swirled by the gray pillar sticking out of the river.

"He probably wouldn't have believed me anyway. Nobody ever does—until it's too late."

The two boys at Jeff's side shrugged their shoulders.

Jeff put Joey's bike back in the grass where he found it. The three headed for town.

A thin, cool wind blew through the rails of the old bridge. Jeff stopped for a moment and listened.

"Help us. Please. Somebody get us out of here."

Jeff shook his head.

"It's one of those things you should know about when you move to a new town."

Or when you cross a bridge.

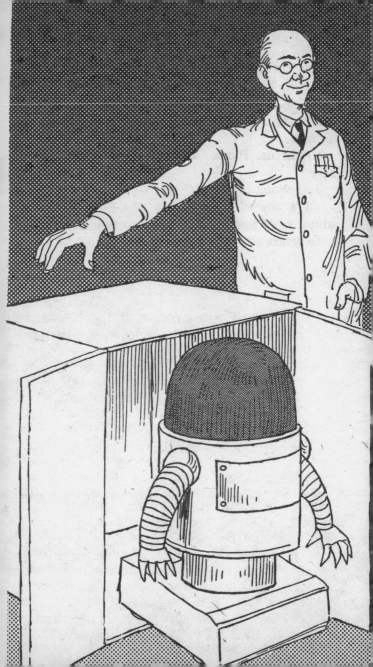

The Robot's Revenge

"May I have your attention, please."

A man in a white lab coat stepped to the center of the small wooden stage. The excited audience in the canvas sideshow tent hushed. They listened to the man, but their eyes were directed to a shiny aluminum box next to him.

The man paid no attention to the box. He looked down at the assembly of men, women, and children, sweeping his gaze across each row, speaking as if he were addressing each individual privately.

"What you are about to see will astound you. A thousand questions will fill your mind. Ten thousand answers will assail you. But only one question will remain when you leave this tent. Only one question will stay in your memory to keep you awake at night, to nag you through the day, and to perplex you to the very day you die. And that question is, *HOW DOES HE DO IT?*"

The man's sudden, unexpected shout startled the audience upright in their chairs. Women gasped. Men's mouths dropped open. And children clung to their mothers' arms, frightened by the thunderous roar.

The man smiled. He nodded slowly as if to reassure his stunned audience that everything was all right.

His brow was very broad. Very little hair remained atop his head. He had a rather narrow chin set far below his arched cheeks which themselves rose to partially conceal his deep, dark eyes. Thin glasses held by shiny wire rims hung suspended on his nose, which was perfectly normal except that it was twisted quite abruptly to one side.

The man's smile was comforting.

"How does he do it?" he whispered, just loudly enough so that the people standing behind the last packed row could hear. "How does he do it?"

He stepped briskly to the metal box. He spread his arms wide in surprise as if he had never seen it before. He slapped an open palm on top of the box. The noise startled the audience once more. Then the man spun about to face the eager faces, keeping his hand on top of the waist-high box.

"Well now you shall see," he said softly.

He leaped away from the box.

"*Open,*" he commanded.

The front of the box swung open slowly. A faint hum from inside was just loud enough to be heard over the rustle of clothes and shuffle of feet as the silent audience moved forward on their seats for a closer look.

"*Presenting Micro-Mite, the world's most amazing robot.*"

Micro-Mite stood inside the box. It fit in the box as snugly as an egg in a carton. It was only a few inches shorter than the box, about the height of a young child. It was made in three separate but connected segments.

The foot of the tiny metal robot was a small platform attached to the center segment of the machine by a thick cylinder. On the bottom of the platform were four spheres, half hidden inside, like roller wheels.

The body segment was a second cylinder, much stouter than the leg. Hanging from each side near the shoulders were two hinged arms which ended in metal fingers.

The head was a dark glass bowl a bit larger than a basketball cut in half.

The audience gasped.

The man spread his arms so that his long lab coat flopped like wings down his sides.

"Micro-Mite. Come."

The small metal device hummed. It glided out of the box on its roller wheels and moved swiftly to the center of the stage where it stopped next to the man.

"Stop," the man said. "Greet your audience, who have come from all over the county to see you."

The robot rolled to the edge of the stage. Children in the audience pulled back as if it were going to topple off the end. But Micro-Mite stopped less than an inch from the three-foot drop.

Ooooh.

Aaahh.

The audience was delighted.

The tiny robot pressed one arm against its torso and extended the other toward the audience. It bowed crisply.

"Just like a butler in the movies," a little girl whispered.

The audience laughed and burst into applause.

"Micro-Mite. Come here."

The roller feet spun Micro-Mite around. It zipped forward and stopped alongside the man again.

The man placed three bright red balls in Micro-Mite's hands.

"How many?" the man asked.

A metallic buzz sounded from Micro-Mite's chest. The sound rose and fell and then became steady.

"Threeee baaaaalllssss."

The robot spoke by modulating the sound of the buzz.

The audience shouted with amazement. They applauded the robot's bright response.

"Juggle the balls, Micro-Mite," the man commanded.

The three red balls flew into the air. They followed one another in a perfect circle as they soared from one hand to another, spinning faster and faster until they were nothing more than a blur of color.

The audience roared its approval when the man ordered his marvelous machine to stop and bow.

The man shouted command after command to the amazing device. It did cartwheels and handstands. It raced around the stage after a mechanical rabbit, chasing it with a long-handled net. When it caught the rabbit, it popped it into a copper kettle on a mock stove. The audience screamed with laughter.

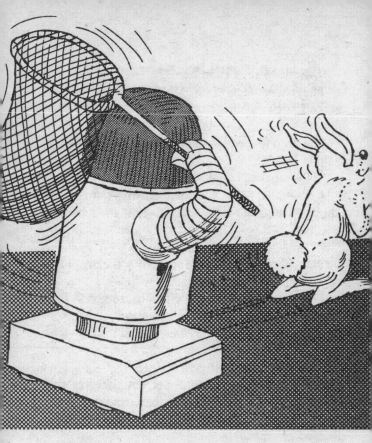

Micro-Mite performed perfectly each and every command the man gave it. It did complex arithmetic problems and announced the answers with its metallic voice. It pulled a child in a coaster wagon. It even picked up the child gently in its short, stiff arms and handed it to its mother who came to the edge of the stage to get her.

With each act the audience's approval grew louder.

After the final trick of the performance, the man called Micro-Mite to his side. He turned to the audience and again looked into the faces of each and every member who stared back, their own eyes fixed on the incredible device called Micro-Mite.

"I know what you are thinking," the man said in a secretive voice. "You can't believe that I have invented a robot so intelligent that it can perform exactly like a human being."

The man threw out his arm and pointed sharply at someone in the back of the room as if he were reading his thoughts.

"You're saying to yourself, it's not a robot. There's a person inside."

The man pointed the accusing finger all around the room as if he could touch everyone and label them doubters.

"Answer me. It's true, isn't it? You think there's someone inside."

The man stepped back and placed his hands on his hips.

"Well?"

The audience murmured. Then sheepish grins appeared on everyone's face. They burst into applause.

"I thought so," the man shouted. He whirled to Micro-Mite and without announcing what he was going to do next, flipped back the dark glass dome-like head like the lid on a kettle.

The audience gasped.

Except for an elaborate network of brightly colored wires, the space between Micro-Mite's body and open dome was empty.

The man clapped the dome closed. With a flourish he unscrewed two shiny nuts on the robot's chest. A panel flopped open like an oven door. Inside was an intricate array of wires and electronic parts. Nothing more.

The audience exploded with spontaneous applause as the man snapped the cover shut and bolted Micro-Mite back together.

He bowed to the audience. At his command, Micro-Mite bowed alongside. Then the man ordered the robot back into the aluminum box.

"I leave you with the same question you brought into the tent," the man said with an air of mystery. *"How does he do it?"*

With that a simple curtain dropped in front of the stage. The performance was over. The audience filed out of the tent, whispering and marvelling among themselves at what they had just seen.

Late that night when the carnival was closed and the midway was as black as tar, a single light shined from a battered house trailer parked away from the others which belonged to the traveling troupe.

The light shined from a crack in a frayed curtain hanging in the window of the trailer. A pair of dark, deep-set eyes peered through the crack into the silent, abandoned gloom.

"Everyone has retired."

The man with the crooked nose let the curtain drop. He covered it with a thick piece of cardboard. The other windows in the dingy trailer were similarly covered. No light could escape. And nobody could look inside.

The aluminum box sat on the floor in the middle of the trailer.

"Please, Krispin. Let me out."

A voice, so weak and muffled that it could scarcely be heard, came from inside the box.

"Oh, shut up."

The man tore off his white coat and flung it at the box. The coat caught on the edge and draped over the top of the box. "Krispin, let me out," he mimicked. "Krispin, give me some food. Krispin, give me some water." The man grimaced at the box, imitating the high-pitched whine of a child pleading for a favor.

"You make me sick," the man screamed at the box.

The box was silent. Then it jiggled. It wiggled.

"Please, Krispin. There's no air."

"Oh, now it's air that you want. Well, that's a new one," the man laughed.

"Please, Krispin. Let me out. I'm suffocating."

"Ho, ho," laughed the man. "I'm sure you are. And as soon as I let you out you'll start in again. 'Krispin, I'm hungry. Krispin, I want some water.'"

The man stormed across the trailer and slammed his hand soundly on top of the box. The noise sounded like a gunshot.

"Well, I'm not going to fall for your cajolery, you stupid little creature. You can spend the night in there for all I care. I'll feed you in the morning when I feed the cat. Ha ha ha."

The man opened a small cupboard over the sink and took down a box of cat food. He rattled it. The box was nearly empty.

"Ho, ho. There may not be enough for both you and the cat, you insufferable twerp. And we wouldn't want kitty to go hungry, now, would we?"

He poured the contents of the box into a bowl on the floor. A mammoth yellow cat plodded on thick paws from its pillow on a couch at the end of the trailer. It sniffed the bowl.

"Go ahead, Pusskin," the man said. He shoved the bowl close to the cat's big nose with his foot. "Our stupid little friend in the box can wait until tomorrow when I go to the store. If he's lucky."

The man with the crooked nose spun around and slammed his hand down on top of the aluminum box again. The noise was deafening. "Ha ha ha," he howled. "You never know when I'm going to drop a bomb on your box, do you? And don't tell me that it hurts your ears. I'm sick of hearing about it." He kicked the box.

The box didn't move. It remained silent.

The man stared at it for a long while. He put his hand to his long, pointed chin. A gray expression of amazement flickered over his dark eyes.

"Well, don't you have anything to say?"

The box was as still as a marble slab in a graveyard.

"Answer me, you idiot. Say something."

The box remained silent.

The man's eyes lighted on the white coat draped over the top of the box.

"The air holes," he gasped.

He tore the coat away. Working feverishly with nervous fingers, he snapped open the front cover of the aluminum box.

Micro-Mite stood inside, nested in its cozy chest like a doll in a Christmas package.

"Come!" the man screamed.

The robot stood stock still.

"You treacherous little creature," the man shouted. "I'll teach you to defy me."

He grabbed the robot and threw it into the dimly lighted room. The tiny machine coasted to a stop against the wall.

"I said *come*," the man shouted.

The robot stood as still as a snowman on a frozen front lawn.

The man dropped to his knees behind the shiny metal creature. He twisted and turned nuts and bolts on Micro-Mite's back.

The cat looked up from its bowl as the man tore the rear cover off the strangely silent machine.

Inside was a tiny dwarf held in place by a tight-fitting harness of leather straps. He was so small that he could fit into the cramped robot and still work the levers and switches inside.

The man with the crooked nose stared at the back of the miniature man. The dwarf didn't move.

The man frantically unsnapped the belts holding the tiny fellow rigid inside the robot. When he undid the last strap the dwarf tumbled to the floor in a heap. He lay there twisted and silent, an expression of terror frozen on his face. He was dead.

Much later a sleepy guard at the carnival midway entrance nodded as the man with the crooked nose drove by in his dented pick-up truck. Behind the truck he towed the trailer. The guard scratched his head and went back to sleep.

Miles away, but before the sun began to turn the eastern sky gray, the man stopped the truck. He backed the trailer to the edge of a dark lake. He dragged the aluminum box from the trailer and shoved it to the lake's shore. A piece of black tape covered the air holes on top of the box.

The man stripped to his shorts. He stepped into the lake and pulled the box after him. He swam to the center of the lake where he untaped the air holes. Water gurgled into the box and it quickly sank to the bottom.

The man swam to shore. He dressed and then drove off without once looking back. The red rail lights of his battered trailer sparkled dimly against the rising sun.

The box lay on the bottom of the lake.

It wiggled.

The front cover opened slowly.

Micro-Mite, lying on his back in the snug box, began to move.

Many days later the man with the crooked nose towed his old trailer into a junkyard. The trailer thumped and banged and the dented, broken-down house sagged awkwardly to one side as if it would fall over any minute.

"Howdy."

A grimy man in coveralls and holding a wrench greeted the man as he stepped out of the pick-up truck.

"What can I do for you?"

"My trailer is broken," the man with the crooked nose said. "Can you fix it?"

The junkyard owner lay down his tools. He crawled under the trailer. In moments he slid back out.

"Nope. Axle is shot. Whole thing is ready to fall over. If I was you, I'd get me a new trailer."

The man with the crooked nose rubbed his chin.

"How much will you give me for it?"

The junk dealer shook his head. "I'll give you twenty-five dollars," he said, "But I'll be sorry in the morning. Ain't worth fifteen."

The man with the crooked nose unhitched the trailer. With the help of the junkyard owner he pushed it into a corner of the lot amid an array of rusty car bodies and broken-down farm machinery.

"Come on in my office and I'll give you a receipt," the junkyard owner said.

The two men stepped into a ramshackle shanty

at the edge of the junkyard.

The man with the crooked nose gasped. "Where did you get that?" he screamed.

The junkyard owner laughed.

"You mean that little space man thing?"

Standing in the corner of the office was Micro-Mite. It was covered with dust and there were rust stains everywhere. Dried mud was packed around the rollers.

"Doesn't that little contraption beat all?" the junkyard owner said. "Found him just this morning 'longside the road on the way to work. Why, it couldn't a been more'n five minutes before you got here."

The man with the crooked nose was speechless. His face had turned ashen gray. His mouth hung open. His fingers trembled.

"And the peculiar thing is, I just passed that place where I found him not five minutes before and he wasn't there," the junkyard owner continued. "Must of dropped out of space. Ha ha ha."

The junkyard man laughed heartily at his own joke.

"Say, is something the matter?" he said.

The man with the crooked nose didn't answer. His knees shook. He looked as if he would drop to the floor any second.

The junkyard man's smile turned serious.

"Say, I better get you a glass of water. You don't look none too good," he said. He was out

the door before the man with the crooked nose
could respond.

"D. . .don't leave me. . .alone. . .with. . .
him," the man with the crooked nose croaked.

Micro-Mite began to hum. The loose fittings
on its rusty body began to vibrate. It began to roll
across the floor toward the terrified man.

"S. . .stay away," the man gasped.

"Y. . .you're dead. You're at the bottom of the lake. Stay away from me. You can't be real."

Micro-Mite continued to roll across the floor.

The man with the crooked nose bolted out the door. He raced across the junkyard driveway. The junkman was nowhere in sight.

Micro-Mite buzzed to a stop at the office door. It raised its arm and grabbed the door handle by its metal fingers. It tore the door from its hinges and threw it across the empty lot into the junkyard.

The man with the crooked nose ran to his pick-up truck. He leaped in. The big yellow cat looked up from the seat next to him. It yawned and went back to sleep.

The robot buzzed and hummed across the dusty lot. It headed straight for the truck.

The man twisted the key. The engine ground but would not start. The man twisted again and again. The engine grumbled like an angry tiger, but it refused to start.

Micro-Mite tore the door off the pick-up truck and threw it over the fence.

The man scrambled across the seat and leaped out the other door. The cat opened an eye and closed it again.

Micro-Mite pursued the man back and forth across the lot, driving him farther and farther back toward the rusting piles of junked vehicles.

The man with the crooked nose slumped against the side of his battered trailer. The door hung open. He gasped for air. He was on the verge of collapse.

Micro-Mite whirred across the lot raising a trail of dust behind him.

The man with the crooked nose jumped into the trailer. He slammed the door.

The lock clicked from the outside. The trailer began to roll. It bumped slowly over the rough ground.

The man with the crooked nose lurched to a window. He threw open the ragged curtain and pressed his nose to the glass.

Micro-Mite was pulling the trailer deep into the lot, far toward the back, down a weed-covered path that hadn't been visited for years.

"No," the man screamed.

He jumped for the door. He pulled on the handle. He banged on it and kicked it with his foot. But the door was closed as tightly as if it had been welded shut.

Micro-Mite shoved the trailer next to a tall stack of old wrecked cars.

"Let me out," the man in the trailer screamed.

But his screams were drowned out by the crashing collapse of the pile of cars which tumbled down over the trailer and buried it completely.

Micro-Mite hummed through the dust and weeds to the front lot. It stopped next to the open passenger door of the pick-up truck. It reached in and tapped the sleeping cat with the tip of a metal finger.

The cat opened one eye. The other eye popped open wide. The cat leaped to its feet and arched its back. Its fur stood out straight as broomstraw. Its mouth dropped open but no sound came out. Its eyes rolled back in its head and its yellow fur turned snow white. It fell over in a heap.

"Now where'd that fellow go?"

The junkyard owner hurried across the empty lot toward the pick-up. He carried a glass of water in his hand, which spilled as he shuffled through the dust.

He stopped at the driver's side of the truck. The door was ripped clean from its hinges.

"What in tarnation's going on around here?" he said. "Looks like some kind of cyclone come through here and ripped off some doors."

He stood in the middle of the lot looking around with a very puzzled expression as he scratched his head and drank the water. "Land o'Goshen if it don't look like it plumb carried off the trailer too."

He peered carefully inside the truck cab. The cat, dead as a doorknob, lay in a white heap on the seat.

"If this ain't the queerest day I ever seen," the junkman said. "If I didn't know better, I'd say this old cat here just saw a ghost."

Micro-Mite whirred and buzzed on the other side of the truck.

"Day in the mornin'," the junkman said as he rushed around to the robot. "The little critter works." He looked around as if he didn't know quite what to do. Then he grinned broadly. He handed the glass to the robot. "Here, young feller, hold this for me for a minute while I pinch myself to see if I ain't dreaming."

Micro-Mite hummed softly. "Aaaat yourrr serrrrvice," it said in a scratchy, metallic voice.

"Don't that beat all? It looks like I own me a real, honest robot," the man said. He pulled a screwdriver from his pocket and unscrewed the panels on the front of Micro-Mite.

"A little fixin' up and some polish and you'll be good as new."

The junkman took the front panel off and lay it gently on the ground. "Always wondered what was inside one of these here things," he said. He stuck his face into the open cavity in Micro-Mite's chest. "Yup. Just like I thought. Nothin' but a lot of wires and electronical stuff."

He opened the back. "Same thing in here," he said. "Nothin' but some wires and these leather straps."

Late that afternoon as the sun was going down, Micro-Mite, polished as bright as a new coffee urn, hummed across the junkyard lot behind the junkman. He clutched a toolbox in one metal hand and carried the man's lunchbox in the other. They got into the man's car together and drove off.

From the weed-covered distant end of the junkyard a low moan carried on the wind.

"Help. Please. Let me out. Please. I need water. I need something to eat. There's no air. There's no air. . ."

And then it was silent.

Don't Go Into Baby's Room

"Mrs. Spizik?"

"Yes?"

"I'm Bonny Clark. You called me to babysit."

A broad smile spread over Abigail Spizik's wrinkled face. She dried her hands on a neatly starched white linen apron tied primly around her waist. She unlatched the screen door and opened it.

"Oh, yes, my dear. The new babysitter. Do come in."

"Thank you."

Bonny Clark hesitated outside the door to the old house at the end of Gravel Pit Road. A rumble of distant thunder and a sudden rush of cold air from inside the house made her shiver. Her blue shorts and faded yellow t-shirt seemed completely inadequate, even though the sky was clear and the sun still shined warmly on her back. She wrapped her arms around herself and rubbed them briskly.

"Quickly, child. Come in."

The old woman stepped back from the open door. Behind her was a long black hall. A candle burning at the end of the hall flickered. A second roll of thunder, closer than the first, echoed down the hall.

Cold wind rushed down the hall. Goosebumps as rough as pinfeathers on a chicken popped up all over Bonny's arms. The wind came from inside the house.

Bonny didn't move.

"I think maybe I. . ."

Mrs. Spizik's arm shot from behind the door. Her dry, scaly hand grasped Bonny tightly by the wrist. The smile was still stretched across her face.

"Come, come, child. Can't you feel the draft? I've left the back door open. If I don't close this door all of my candles will blow out."

"C. .candles?"

Bonny stepped reluctantly into the hallway.

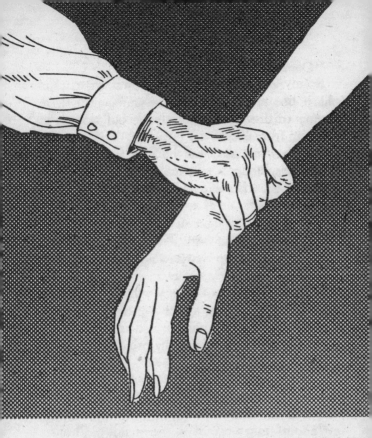

Mrs. Spizik slammed the door quickly behind her. The wind stopped but the air was still as chilly as night.

"You see. It makes such a draft."

Thunder rumbled again. Bonny looked up to the ceiling. The sound seemed to come from directly over her head.

"My, my, it sounds as if we're in for a storm."

"But there are no clouds. . ."

"Come, come, my dear."

Mrs. Spizik tugged at Bonny's wrist. Her sharp, bony fingers cut into the young girl's flesh. Bonny winced. She followed the old woman to avoid more pain.

The two walked down the long, dark hallway. They came to a closed door at the end. Mrs. Spizik cocked her ear to the door. "We can go in," she said.

A tidy, pleasant kitchen was on the other side. Bubbling on an old-fashioned wood stove was a large teapot. Its top clattered noisily as clouds of steam popped it up and down.

Mrs. Spizik let go of Bonny's wrist. "Sit down, my dear. I'll make us a nice cup of tea."

Bonny relaxed. A thin smile struggled over her lips. Her eyes brightened. She breathed a careful sigh of relief.

"Thank you. That would be nice."

A roll of thunder echoed from above. It sounded like heavy furniture being moved across a wooden floor upstairs in the quaint old house.

The kitchen was warm from the glow of the stove, but the goosebumps appeared on Bonny's arms again as the thunder died away.

"Well, sit, dearie."

Bonny pulled a heavy chair from the table.

"Thank you."

Mrs. Spizik poured two cups of steaming water through a silver strainer filled with tea leaves. She passed a cup to Bonny.

"Sugar?"

"Yes, please."

The old woman passed a china sugar bowl to Bonny.

"Take all you like, my dear. Sweets for the sweet."

A sharp crash of thunder rocked the room. The sugar bowl shook in Bonny's hand. Sugar spilled onto the lace tablecloth.

"Oh, I'm sorry."

Mrs. Spizik didn't notice. Her attention was on the ceiling. She stared up with empty eyes. Her bright smile was gone.

"Drink your tea, dearie. It's time."

"Time?"

The old woman got up from the table. She put her teacup on the sink. She stepped behind Bonny's chair and put her cold hands on Bonny's shoulders.

"Yes, child. Cecil wants to meet you."

"Cecil?"

The old woman said nothing. She dug her fingers into Bonny's shoulders. Bonny pulled away.

"I said, *come,* child."

Bonny rose from the chair. She pulled away from the old woman's claws.

"I. .I think I'd like to call my mother. . ."

Thunder rocked the room. The old woman lifted her eyes to the ceiling.

"Coming, Cecil. I'm coming."

She pushed Bonny through the doorway back into the hall. With her sharp grip once more clutched around Bonny's wrist, she pulled the terrified girl to a stairway and forced her to climb.

"I want to call my mother. Please. . ."

"Coming, Cecil."

The old woman disregarded Bonny's pleas.

A dark oak door at the top of the stairs rattled as the thunder boomed again. The thunder was not outside at all. It was coming from the room.

"We're here, Cecil," the old woman said.

She pushed open the door cautiously. She stuck her face into the room.

"Cecil?"

The room was silent.

The old woman jerked Bonny into the room and quickly closed the door behind them.

In the center of the room was an elaborate bassinet. It was decorated from top to bottom with blue satin bows and covered with cloudy blue chiffon netting.

When Bonny saw it she relaxed.

"Then there *is* a baby," she said.

The old woman stared coldly at the young girl. "Of course there's a baby," she hissed.

"I. .I'm sorry," Bonny said. "I guess I was a little scared and I. . ."

"Sssh. You'll wake him."

Bonny stood respectfully quiet as the old woman tiptoed to the gay crib in the middle of the room.

"Your new babysitter is here, Cecil," she whispered through the folds of colorful cloth draping the crib. "You won't be needing me any longer."

Bonny looked at the old woman with curiosity.

The old woman turned to Bonny. A strange smile spread over her face. She opened her arms and walked slowly toward Bonny.

"Now it's your turn," the old woman said.

Bonny turned toward the door. It was locked.

"Come, dearie. It only takes a moment. Come to me. It's time for me to go."

The old woman advanced slowly toward

Bonny. Bonny couldn't move. The woman's arms enfolded her. They were as cold as ice. They wrapped tightly around the girl.

Bonny opened her mouth to scream.

The woman squeezed so hard that Bonny couldn't breath. She squeezed tighter and tighter.

Suddenly the old woman relaxed her grip. Her arms fell to her sides. A frightened expression of terror crossed her face.

A beautiful young woman in a floor-length gown stepped out of the old woman's open arms. Her face was bone white. Jet black hair parted in the middle of her head fell in long shiny waves over her shoulders. The woman smiled a thin smile at the old woman.

"It's time for me to go now," she said in a hollow, faraway voice. "Look after Cecil," she said. "He's really a good baby, once you get to know him."

The young woman turned toward the door. She glided over the floor as if she were floating on a cloud. She began to fade as she reached the door like smoke on a breezy day. She passed right through the closed oak door and was gone.

Bonny stood silently next to the baby's cradle. Her eyes were open wide. Her mouth moved to speak.

"Help me," she said. "Help me."

She raised her hand in front of her face. It was dry and scaly and as gray as death. She began to cry softly.

The room shook with thunder. Bonny put her gnarled, bony hand on the cradle and rocked it gently.

"Ssssh. Sleep, Cecil. Everything is all right. Your new babysitter is here. Her name is. . .her name is Bonny."

The House on Pearl Street

The moment Evan entered the big gray house on Pearl Street he knew it was a mistake.

The floors sagged terribly. Evan skirted around the edge of the room to reach the door leading to the back of the house. The front door had blown shut and locked behind him the minute he stepped inside the abandoned house.

"I wish I never found that stupid shortcut through the woods," Evan said. His voice rumbled in the empty room.

The floor creaked. Evan kept his back pressed to the wall as he inched toward the door.

"That better lead outside is all I can say," he said.

A cool breeze blew across the room. It brushed over his bare legs. Compared to the heat of the day baking the dry fields surrounding the house, the breeze felt good.

Evan stopped next to a large window which reached nearly from the floor to the ceiling. It was covered by a very dusty drape. A trickle of light leaked into the room through a tear in the drape.

Evan hooked his finger into the hole and pulled the drape an inch from the glass. He stared through the opening onto the lawn surrounding the house. The lawn was perfectly white.

Evan's eyes opened as wide as doorknobs.

"That's *snow*."

Evan threw open the ragged drapes, heedless of the heavy coat of dust clinging to them.

The yard, the woods, and the meadow as far as he could see were covered with a deep blanket of snow. Sparkling patterns of frost dressed the windowpanes, magnifying the sight and distorting it so that it looked as if the trees were made of melting plastic.

Evan put his palm against the glass. It was

bitter cold. A tiny stream of water ran down the pane as the ice under his hand melted. It dripped onto the floor punching little craters in the dust.

The floor behind Evan creaked and moaned. The hair on the back of his neck stood up straight. He let the drape drop and turned very slowly to face the empty room.

It wasn't empty. Paintings graced the walls. Furniture stood everywhere. A dusty rug covered the floor. None of it had been in the room when Evan first entered.

The terrified boy raced for the door at the back of the room. He grabbed the knob with both hands and tugged it open.

A giant as tall as the doorway stood on the other side. A tattered, ragged black suit hung in dusty shreds from his angular, rail-thin frame. Gray, bloodless hands hung like gnarled twigs from the sleeves. They twitched nervously as if clutching something unseen inside their dry, bony grip.

The man's face was as gray as the dust which lay everywhere in the house. Great cavernous sockets, sunk deep beneath a thick, protruding forehead, hid tiny white eyes which blinked in surprise at the petrified youth frozen like a statue in the open doorway.

The man's mouth hung open, twisted crooked as if the jaw were unhooked on one side. Black teeth glistened inside his mouth, which was also gray and colorless as a hornet's nest.

The man reached for Evan with sharp fingers.

"Maaaaa," Evan screamed.

There was no place to run. The front door was locked. The giant blocked the only other door.

"The window," Evan shouted.

He ran toward the window.

The man stepped into the room after him.

"Get away from me! Get away from me!" Evan screamed.

The giant creature lumbered forward in a halting, uneven gait. One foot dragged in the dust leaving a crooked line across the floor.

Evan grabbed a dining room chair. He swung it furiously at the advancing giant.

"Get away from me."

The man kept coming.

Evan scooted around the scattered pieces of furniture. He worked his way carefully toward the window. He held the chair in front of him like a shield. When he was within easy reach of the window, he raised the chair over his head and aimed.

"Pssst. Don't break the window."

Evan's arms froze in place. He held the heavy chair over his head. He stared at the giant's mouth. It hung open crooked. It hadn't moved.

"Over here, kid. In the wall."

Evan let the chair drop slowly to the floor. A panel in the wall opposite the window was open. A capped head covered with shiny, curly black hair, with a face split ear to ear by a bright smile, stuck out of the open panel. It was a boy about Evan's age and size.

"Duck in here before he gets you," the boy said.

Evan didn't stop to think. He let go of the chair and clambered across the furniture to the other side of the room.

The giant stopped. He stood dumbly by the window as if thinking it were a very difficult task. Then he resumed his plodding pursuit of Evan.

Evan reached the open panel first. The boy on the other side grabbed him and pulled him through.

The instant Evan was safely through the panel the boy slammed it shut and dropped a heavy board across it, locking it securely in place.

The giant's thumping, one-step shuffle stopped on the other side of the wall. It waited for a very long time.

"We're o.k.," the curly-headed youth said.

Then his smile faded. "For now, anyway," he added.

Evan was still too stunned to speak. He blinked as he looked around. He was in a narrow tunnel between two walls. It was dark and dingy. Cobwebs hung from every corner. The only light came from a flickering candle which the boy held.

"Come on," the boy said. "Follow me."

Evan followed dumbly.

"It's a secret passage," the boy said. He led Evan cautiously through the labyrinth which twisted and turned deep inside the strange house on Pearl Street.

"Through here."

Evan followed the boy. They stepped through another open wall panel into another room.

"Oooh. A new boy."

The room was well lighted. Candles and kerosene lamps basked the room in a warm glow. The windows were tightly draped. There was no dust. No cobwebs hung in the corners. The furniture, an abundance of elegant, polished wood, bright shiny glass, and exquisite cloth, shouted in gay colors. The room was lived in.

In the midst of it all stood a group of children.

A small, blond-haired girl with curls hanging like long springs on each side of her pert face was the youngest, perhaps six or seven years old. Another girl, tall, with short, bobbed hair, was the oldest. She was in her teens. Eight others, boys and girls of varying ages and all dressed quite unalike, made up the rest of the group.

Each of them wore a costume. The little blond girl wore a long blue gown decorated with satin ribbons which hung nearly to the floor. Shiny patent leather shoes glistened as black as polished coal on her feet.

The boy who rescued Evan from the giant wore knickers, knee-length pants with tight stockings from the knee down. A flat cap sat at a jaunty angle on his head. His plain white shirt had a short, stiff collar.

All the others had equally as interesting clothes. Compared to Evan's cut-offs, t-shirt, and worn-down running shoes, they looked as if they were from a history book.

"Is this a party?"

The group giggled and laughed at Evan's simple, earnest question.

Evan moved nervously from foot to foot, uncomfortable and feeling out of place.

"Well, is it?"

The snickering and giggling stopped. The teenage girl put her hand on Evan's arm. Her hand was as cold as the frost he had felt on the window.

"No," the girl said. "But we wished it was."

"The man downstairs, the one that was chasing you. He's real," the curly-headed boy said. He gestured to the others in the group who surrounded Evan with great interest as if he had dropped in from outer space. "And so are we," he added.

Evan was puzzled. He rubbed the top of his head with the back of his hand. "I don't get it," he said.

The little girl with the curls took Evan by the hand and led him to a window. She pulled back the heavy drape.

The lawn and trees outside were covered with bright, crisp, gold and yellow leaves of autumn. Red apples hung in abundance from the branches of a nearby tree. The meadows surrounding the house were tan with a cover of dried grass.

"But it's still summer. . ."

Then Evan remembered the snow outside the downstairs window.

"It's all the seasons here," the boy said.

The group nodded their heads sadly.

A spine tingling chill shot down Evan's back. His mouth fell open. Tears formed in the corners of his eyes.

"You're ghosts."

The gathered circle of children nodded again.

Evan jumped away from them.

"But not me," he shouted. "Not me!"

The group nodded.

"No," Evan screamed. "I'm not even dead. I'm alive. I was taking a short cut through the woods and I found this old place, that's all. But I'm alive."

The little girl sniffled. She shook her head slowly from side to side.

The curly-headed boy advanced toward Evan, who was too stunned to move. The boy put a reassuring hand on Evan's shoulder.

"You're alive now," the boy said. "But soon you'll be just like us. It's inevitable."

Evan wrinkled his brow.

"You can't escape it," the teen-age girl said. "No matter how much you want to, you'll be like us soon."

"I don't believe it," Evan said sharply. "This is a stupid joke or game or something." He looked each of the strangely dressed youths straight in their faces. "And I don't think it's funny. Now tell me how to get out of here so I can go home."

"We all tried to get out," the curly-haired boy said. "I know I did. I found this house just like you did. It was a long, long time ago. When I stepped into the big room downstairs the door blew shut." The boy dropped his chin to his chest. "I've been here ever since."

The others nodded.

"What about that big, that big *thing* down

there?'' Evan demanded. "That ugly creep with
the rotten clothes and the crummy skin and, and,
and what about *him?* Who is he?''

Evan was shaking. His eyes fluttered. His teeth
chattered.

"He's the one that gets you.''

Every candle in the room began to flicker.
Some went out. The group of kids raced for the
corners of the room. Some bolted through the
secret panel and vanished.

"It's him. He's coming to get you.''

The curly-haired boy was the last to disappear.
He stuck his head out of an open panel in the
wall. He shook it helplessly. "Run. Run if you
can. There's nothing we can do to help. *Run.*''

And then Evan was alone.

A thumping, shuffling noise stopped outside
the door. The door handle turned. Evan stood on
flat feet twisting and turning his head around the
room, frantically looking for a place to hide or
escape.

The door flew open. The creature, the tall, ugly
man with the tattered clothes, filled the doorway.
His arms reached out in front of him. His gray,
spindly fingers clutched at the air. He took a step
and was in the room.

Evan dashed around a large table. He pounded
on the walls. The walls were as solid as tree
trunks.

"Where are you?'' he shouted. "Where is the
panel that opens up?''

There was no response from the other side of the wall. The giant shuffled on ungainly legs across the room after Evan.

Evan beat on the walls. He ran up and down the side of the room pounding and listening, but there was no hollow sound or voice in reply.

The giant closed the gap between him and Evan.

Evan made a break for it. He raced around the table and dashed for the open door. He bounded through it into the darkness on the other side. He plunged headlong down a steep, narrow flight of steps, tumbling like a falling rag doll to the floor at the bottom.

He sat up and shook his head groggily. A thump at the top of the stairs grabbed his attention. The giant was there. He blocked the light coming from the room, turning the long stairway into night.

Evan groped for a way out. Dust choked his lungs. Cobwebs wrapped around his face in sticky masks. Sharp boards and rough walls gnawed at his bare knees.

"Maaaaa!"

His scream echoed eerily through the darkness as he stumbled along with outstretched arms, feeling for a door, a window, anything to escape from the awful house.

The giant's limping thunder followed him. The sound grew closer. Evan was out of breath. His heart pounded. He was weak. He leaned against an unseen wall, gasping for air.

"You can't get away."

"It's impossible to escape him."

"We all tried."

Voices, the voices of the children came from the other side of the wall.

"Where are you? How do I get in there?" Evan pleaded. He pounded the wall with his fists. Nails tore his flesh. "Open a panel. Please let me in. He's almost here."

The giant bumped and thudded against the walls of the narrow passage. His foot dragged across the floor. Evan couldn't move.

Suddenly the thing was there. His long, cold, bony fingers clutched Evan by the arm. He pulled the screaming, kicking boy toward him.

Evan mustered the last of his strength and courage. He jerked away. He was free.

Mindless that he couldn't see a meter in front of his face, Evan ran at a gallop through the dark corridor. All along the way voices in the wall whispered to him as he passed.

"You'll never get away. We all tried. He'll get you in the end. He always does."

"No!" Evan screamed.

He ran full force into an unseen door at the end of the passage. It burst open, flying from its hinges under the powerful impact of the fleeing, fear-driven boy.

Evan stumbled off the edge of a porch and tumbled to the grass. The smell of warm, moist earth calmed him. He wrapped his fingers tightly around clumps of long, juicy green grass. A warm sun beat down on his back. He rolled over. The bright sun beat down to warm his fear-frozen body with the tender touch of summer. "I made it," he gasped. "I made it."

Evan sat up unsteadily. He shook his head. Vague, unsure memories danced strangely on the edge of his mind. He blinked his eyes. He held a tuft of grass to his nose. It was warm and green and smelled the way his own backyard did after he mowed.

Evan turned. The house on Pearl Street, as gray as a mound of dust, baked in the sun. The back door swung slowly back and forth, hanging on a single hinge. Evan rubbed his eyes.

"I know it wasn't a dream," he said. "But what was it?"

He stood and dusted himself off. Cobwebs clung to him everywhere. He was covered with dust from head to foot and every patch of bare skin was scuffed or bruised. He started for the overgrown lane that passed in front of the dreary house.

"I don't think I'll ever understand what happened," he said. "But I made it, and that's all that counts."

A thump on the porch froze him in mid-step. The hair on his arms and legs stood up as goosebumps covered him from head to toe. Bitter cold wind blew over him.

The giant was on the porch. It was outside. It was still after him.

Evan couldn't move his legs. His feet were planted firmly on the soft, springy grass of summer, but they wouldn't move.

A long black shadow passed over Evan. His eyes rolled back in their sockets as the giant wrapped his ragged, bony arms around him.

The giant dragged Evan back to the house. Evan was silent. He hung limp in the cruel grasp of the dread creature.

They vanished inside the house on Pearl Street.

Everything was just as it was before. The sun blazed on cool green grass. Bugs hummed in the shadows of the strange house. Birds swooped and skimmed the air overhead. Only one thing was different. The door was open.

Now the creature could get out.